I0606820

Stephen Phillips, und Andere

Primavera

Poems by Four Authors

Stephen Phillips, und Andere

Primavera
Poems by Four Authors

ISBN/EAN: 9783744771054

Printed in Europe, USA, Canada, Australia, Japan

Cover: Foto ©Andreas Hilbeck / pixelio.de

More available books at **www.hansebooks.com**

PRIMAVERA: POEMS, BY FOUR AUTHORS.

OXFORD: PUBLISHED BY B. H. BLACKWELL, BROAD STREET.

MDCCCXC.

*For permission to print the Poems numbered V., X.,
and XIV., and that numbered VI., the Authors are indebted
to the Editor of "The Oxford Magazine" and the Editor of
"Temple Bar."*

POEMS.

I.

NO Muse will I invoke ; for she is fled !
    Lo ! where she sits, breathing, yet all but
        dead.
She loved the heavens of old, she thought them
        fair ;
And dream'd of Gods in Tempe's golden air.
For her the wind had voice, the sea its cry ;
She deem'd heroic Greece could never die.
Breathless was she, to think what nymphs might
        play
In clear green depths, deep-shaded from the day ;
She thought the dim and inarticulate god
Was beautiful, nor knew she man a sod ;
But hoped what seem'd might not be all untrue,
And fear'd to look beyond the eternal blue.
But now the heavens are bared of dreams divine.
Still murmurs she, like Autumn, *This was mine !*

How should she face the ghastly, jarring Truth,
That questions all, and tramples without ruth?
And still she clings to Ida of her dreams,
And sobs, *Ah! let the world be what it seems!*
Then the shy nymph shall softly come again;
The world, once more, make music for her pain.
For, sitting in the dim and ghostly night,
She fain would stay the strong approach of light;
While later bards cleave to her, and believe
That in her sorrow she can still conceive!
Oh, let her dream; still lovely is her sigh:
Oh, rouse her not, or she shall surely die.

STEPHEN PHILLIPS.

II.

YOUTH.

WHEN life begins anew,
    And Youth, from gathering flowers,
From vague delights, rapt musings, twilight hours,
Turns restless, seeking some great deed to do,
To sum his foster'd dreams; when that fresh
        birth
Unveils the real, the throng'd and spacious Earth,
And he awakes to those more ample skies,
By other aims and by new powers possess'd :
How deeply, then, his breast
Is fill'd with pangs of longing ! how his eyes
Drink in the enchanted prospect ! Fair it lies
Before him, with its plains expanding vast,
Peopled with visions, and enrich'd with dreams ;
Dim cities, ancient forests, winding streams,
Places resounding in the famous past,
A kingdom ready to his hand !
How like a bride Life seems to stand
In welcome, and with festal robes array'd !
He feels her loveliness pervade

And pierce him with inexplicable sweetness;
And, in her smiles delighting, and the fires
Of his own pulses, passionate soul!
Measures his strength by his desires,
And the wide future by their fleetness,
As his thought leaps to the long-distant goal.

So eagerly across that unknown span
Of years he gazes : what, to him,
Are bounds and barriers, tales of Destiny,
Death, and the fabled impotence of man ?
Already, in his marching dream,
Men at his sun-like coming seem
As with an inspiration stirr'd, and he
To kindle with new thoughts degenerate nations,
In sordid cares immersed so long;
Thrill'd with ethereal exultations
And a victorious expectancy,
Even such as swell'd the breasts of Bacchus'
          throng,
When that triumphal burst of joy was hurl'd
Upon the wondering world;
When from the storied, sacred East afar,
Down Indian gorges clothed in green,
With flower-rein'd tigers and with ivory car
He came, the youthful god;
Beautiful Bacchus, ivy-crown'd, his hair
Blown on the wind, and flush'd limbs bare,

And lips apart, and radiant eyes,
And ears that caught the coming melodies,
As wave on wave of revellers swept abroad ;
Wreathed with vine-leaves, shouting, trampling
     onwards,
With toss'd timbrel and loud tambourine.

Alas ! the disenchanting years have roll'd
On hearts and minds becoming cold :
Mirth is gone from us ; and the world is old.

O bright new-comer, fill'd with thoughts of joy,
Joy to be thine amid these pleasant plains,
Know'st thou not, child, what surely coming pains
Await thee, for that eager heart's annoy ?
Misunderstanding, disappointment, tears,
Wrong'd love, spoil'd hope, mistrust and ageing
     fears,
Eternal longing for one perfect friend,
And unavailing wishes without end ?
Thou proud and pure of spirit, how must thou
     bear
To have thine infinite hates and loves confined,
School'd, and despised ? How keep unquench'd
     and free
'Mid others' commerce and economy
Such ample visions, oft in alien air
Tamed to the measure of the common kind ?

How hard for thee, swept on, forever hurl'd
From hour to hour, bewilder'd and forlorn,
To move with clear eyes and with steps secure,
To keep the light within, to fitly scorn
Those all too possible and easy goals,
Trivial ambitions of soon-sated souls !
And, patient in thy purpose, to endure
The pity and the wisdom of the world.

Vain, vain such warning to those happy ears !
Disturb not their delight !   By unkind powers
Doom'd to keep pace with the relentless Hours,
He, too, ere long, shall feel Earth's glory change;
Familiar names shall take an accent strange,
A deeper meaning, a more human tone ;
No more pass'd by, unheeded or unknown,
The things that then shall be beheld through
          tears.

Yet, O just Nature, thou
Who, if men's hearts be hard, art always mild ;
O fields and streams, and places undefiled,
Let your sweet airs be ever on his brow,
Remember still your child.
Thou too, O human world, if old desires,
If thoughts, not alien once, can move thee now,
Teach him not yet that idly he aspires
Where thou hast fail'd ; not soon let it be plain,

That all who seek in thee for nobler fires,
For generous passion, spend their hopes in vain :
Lest that insidious Fate, foe of mankind,
Who ever waits upon our weakness, try
With whispers his unnerved and faltering mind,
Palsy his powers ; for she has spells to dry,
Like the March blast, his blood, turn flesh to
       stone,
And, conjuring action with necessity,
Freeze the quick will, and make him all her own.

Come, then, as ever, like the Wind at morning !
Joyous, O Youth, in the aged world renew
Freshness to feel the eternities around it,
Rains, stars, and clouds, light and the sacred dew.
The strong sun shines above thee :
That strength, that radiance bring !
If Winter come to Winter,
When shall men hope for Spring ?

LAURENCE BINYON.

III.

'TIS my twentieth year: dim, now, youth
    stretches behind me ;
Breaking fresh at my feet, lies, like an ocean,
    the world.
And despised seem, now, those quiet fields I have
    travell'd :
Eager to thee I turn, Life, and thy visions of joy.
Fame I see, with her wreath, far off approaching
    to crown me ;
Love, whose starry eyes fever my heart with
    desire :
And impassion'd I yearn for the future, all
    unconscious,
Ah, poor dreamer ! what ills life in its circle
    enfolds.
Not more restless the boy, whose eager, confident
    bosom
The wide, unknown sea fills with a hunger to
    roam.
Often beside the surge of the desolate ocean he
    paces ;

Ingrate, dreams of a sky brighter, serener than his.

Passionate soul! light holds he a mother's tear-
    ful entreaties,

Lightly leaves he behind all the sad faces of
    home;

Never again, perchance, to behold them; lost in
    the tempest,

Or on some tropic shore dying in fever and pain!

MANMOHAN GHOSE.

IV.

TESTAMENTUM AMORIS.

I CANNOT raise my eyelids up from sleep,
  But I am visited with thoughts of you ;
Slumber has no refreshment half so deep
As the sweet morn, that wakes my heart anew.

I cannot put away life's trivial care,
But you straightway steal on me with delight :
My purest moments are your mirror fair ;
My deepest thought finds you the truth most bright.

You are the lovely regent of my mind,
The constant sky to my unresting sea ;
Yet, since 'tis you that rule me, I but find
A finer freedom in such tyranny.

Were the world's anxious kingdoms govern'd so,
Lost were their wrongs, and vanish'd half their
        woe !

LAURENCE BINYON.

V.

AMAVIMUS, AMAMUS, AMABIMUS.

PERSEPHONE, Persephone !
　　Still I fancy I can see
Thee amid the daffodils.
Golden wealth thy basket fills ;
Golden blossoms at thy breast ;
Golden hair that shames the West ;
Golden sunlight round thy head !
Ah ! the golden years have fled ;
Thee have reft, and me have left
Here alone, thy loss to mourn.

Persephone, Persephone !
Still I fancy I can see
Her, as white and still she lies :
Death has woo'd and won his prize.
White the blossoms at her breast ;
White and still her face at rest ;
White the moonbeams round her head.
Ah ! the wintry years have fled ;

Comfort lent and patience sent,
And my grief is easier borne.

Persephone, Persephone !
Still in dreams thou com'st to me ;
Every night art at my side,
Half my bride, and half Death's bride !
Golden blossoms at thy breast ;
Golden hair that shames the West ;
Golden sunlight circling thee !
Half of gold the lone years flee :
Night is glad, though day is sad,
Till I go where thou art gone.

ARTHUR S. CRIPPS.

VI.

TO A LOST LOVE.

I CANNOT look upon thy grave,
  Though there the rose is sweet :
Better to hear the long wave wash
  These wastes about my feet !

Shall I take comfort ?   Dost thou live
  A spirit, though afar,
With a deep hush about thee, like
  The stillness round a star ?

Oh, thou art cold !   In that high sphere
  Thou art a thing apart,
Losing in saner happiness
  This madness of the heart.

And yet, at times, thou still shalt feel
  A passing breath, a pain ;
Disturb'd, as though a door in heaven
  Had oped and closed again.

And thou shalt shiver, while the hymns,
  The solemn hymns, shall cease;
A moment half remember me:
  Then turn away to peace.

But oh, for evermore thy look,
  Thy laugh, thy charm, thy tone,
Thy sweet and wayward earthliness,
  Dear trivial things, are gone!

Therefore I look not on thy grave,
  Though there the rose is sweet;
But rather hear the loud wave wash
  These wastes about my feet.

                    STEPHEN PHILLIPS.

VII.

RAYMOND AND IDA.

RAYMOND.

DEAREST, that sit'st in dreams,
  Through the window look, this way.
How changed and desolate seems
  The world, Ida, to-day!
Heavy and low the sky is glooming:
  Winter is coming!

IDA.

My dreaming heart is stirr'd:
  Sadly the winter comes!
The wind is loud: how weird,
  Heard in these darken'd rooms!
Speak to me, Raymond; ease this dread:
  I am afraid, afraid.

RAYMOND.

Love, what is this?   Like snow
  Thy cheeks feel, snow they wear.

B

What ails my darling so ?
  What is it thou dost hear ?
Close, close, thy soft arms cling to mine :
  Tears on thy lashes shine.

IDA.

Hark ! love, the wind wails by
  The wet October trees,
Swaying them mournfully :
  The wet leaves shower and cease.
And hark ! how blows the weary rain,
  Against the shaken pane

RAYMOND.

Ah, yes, the world is drear
  Outside ; there is no rest.
But what can Ida fear,
  Shelter'd upon my breast ?
Heed not the storm-blast, beating wild
  I love thee, love thee, child.

IDA.

Thy breath is in my hair,
  Thy kisses on my cheek ;
Yet I scarce feel them there :
  Faintly I hear thee speak.
My heart is dreaming far away,
  In some sad, future day.

RAYMOND AND IDA.

RAYMOND.

The future ? In the mist
  Of years what dost thou see ?
O let that dark land rest :
  Come back, come back to me !
Look up ! How fix'd and vacant seem
  Thine eyes ; so deep they dream.

IDA.

To leave the blessed light :
  Cold in the grave to lie !
No voice, no human sight :
  Darkness and apathy !
To die ! 'tis hard, ere youth is o'er ;
  But ah, to love no more !

RAYMOND.

What dream is this, alas !
  O, if but for my sake,
Wake, darling ; let this pass :
  Ida, dear Ida, wake !
I cannot bear to see those tears :
  Thy sad tones hurt my ears.

IDA.

Will he forget me, then,
  When I am gone away ?

'Twere best : to give him pain,
   Let not my memory stay.
But O, even there, in Hades dim,
   I would remember him.

RAYMOND.

Thou griev'st thyself in vain :
   Sweet love, be comforted.
Come, leave this world of rain ;
   To the bright hearth turn thy head.
We have our fireside still, the same :
   How cheerful is the flame !

Though darkness round us press ;
   Though wild, without, it blows ;
Here sit thee, while thy face
   In the happy firelight glows :
Clasp'd in my arms, lie tranquil here ;
   And listen, Ida dear.

As, from that outlook chill,
   The glad hearth meets our sight,
A charm for every ill
   We bear, a charm of might.
Ah, 'gainst its power not death shall stay !
   Know'st thou it, darling, say ?

Thou smilest ! Joy, I see,
 Dawns in thine eyes again :
Those cheeks of ivory
 Their own sweet bloom regain.
Thou know'st that heavenly charm ;
  how well,
 Thy happy kisses tell !

MANMOHAN GHOSE.

VIII.

PSYCHE.

SHE is not fair, as some are fair,
      Cold as the snow, as sunshine gay :
On her clear brow, come grief what may,
She suffers not too stern an air ;
But, grave in silence, sweet in speech,
Loves neither mockery nor disdain ;
Gentle to all, to all doth teach
The charm of deeming nothing vain.

She join'd me: and we wander'd on ;
And I rejoiced, I cared not why,
Deeming it immortality
To walk with such a soul alone.
Primroses pale grew all around,
Violets, and moss, and ivy wild ;
Yet, drinking sweetness from the ground,
I was but conscious that she smiled.

The wind blew all her shining hair
From her sweet brows; and she, the while,
Put back her lovely head, to smile
On my enchanted spirit there.

Jonquils and pansies round her head
Gleam'd softly; but a heavenlier hue
Upon her perfect cheek was shed,
And in her eyes a purer blue.

There came an end to break the spell;
She murmur'd something in my ear;
The words fell vague, I did not hear,
And ere I knew, I said farewell;
And homeward went, with happy heart
And spirit dwelling in a gleam,
Rapt to a Paradise apart,
With all the world become a dream.

Yet now, too soon, the world's strong strife
Breaks on me pitiless again;
The pride of passion, hopes made vain,
The wounds, the weariness, of life.
And losing that forgetful sphere,
For some less troubled world I sigh,
If not divine, more free, more clear,
Than this poor, soil'd humanity.

But when, in trances of the night,
Wakeful, my lonely bed I keep,
And linger at the gate of Sleep,
Fearing, lest dreams deny me light;

Her image comes into the gloom,
With her pale features moulded fair,
Her breathing beauty, morning bloom,
My heart's delight, my tongue's despair.

With loving hand she touches mine,
Showers her soft tresses on my brow,
And heals my heart, I know not how,
Bathing me with her looks divine.
She beckons me ; and I arise ;
And, grief no more remembering,
Wander again with rapturous eyes
Through those enchanted lands of Spring.

Then, as I walk with her in peace,
I leave this troubled air below,
Where, hurrying sadly to and fro,
Men toil, and strain, and cannot cease :
Then, freed from tyrannous Fate's control,
Untouch'd by years or grief, I see
Transfigured in that child-like soul
The soil'd soul of humanity.

LAURENCE BINYON.

IX.

A LAMENT.

OVER thy head, in joyful wanderings
    Through heaven's wide spaces, free,
Birds fly with music in their wings ;
  And from the blue, rough sea
  The fishes flash and leap ;
There is a life of loveliest things
  O'er thee, so fast asleep.

In the deep West the heavens grow heavenlier,
  Eve after eve ; and still
The glorious stars remember to appear ;
  The roses on the hill
  Are fragrant as before :
Only thy face, of all that's dear,
  I shall see nevermore !

MANMOHAN GHOSE.

UNIVERSITY OF CALIFORNIA

X.

UNDINES OF DIVERSE DAYS.

I.

THÉ eyes of heaven were on her bent,
  In a rapture of loving wonderment,
As her song with the nightingale's was blent :
And one yearn'd for a love, and one sigh'd for a
    soul !

Moonlight and starlight alike seemed cold,
As their silver glanced on her locks of gold ;
And the dream on her face was a dream of old,
Whose sorrow no sunrise might smile away.

I read her yearning and weary smile,
As her song rang sadder and sadder the while,
With its weird refrain of a magic isle,
Where some might have rest, but never might she !

She, the darling of Sky and Stream,
She was but as wind, or as wave, or as dream,
To play for a while in life's glory and gleam :
But what would be left at the end of the day ?

II.

The sun smiles down upon her distress
With a tyrant smile most pitiless,
As she stitches away in her tatter'd dress,
With a song on her lips, that sinks in a sigh.

Yet, scorning her dusty window pane,
For all his pride, in love he is fain
Soft gold on her golden hair to rain ;
But no sunlight may soften that soulless stare.

I read her yearning and weary sigh,
And the eyes that would be, but are not, dry ;
And I catch the voice of that voiceless cry
For a moment to rest, for a moment to weep.

She, the darling of Want and Woe,
Why was she sent, save to work and to go
With feet that will ever more weary grow ?
Whither ? she has not a moment to care !

The Undine of olden days, I read,
By the love of a soul from her trammels was
       freed :
Knows there another such dolorous need ?
Sure on the earth lingers yet such a soul !

ARTHUR S. CRIPPS.

XI.

A DREAM.

M Y dead love came to me, and said,
   ' God gives me one hour's rest,
To spend with thee on earth again :
   How shall we spend it best ? '

' Why, as of old,' I said ; and so
   We quarrell'd, as of old :
But, when I turn'd to make my peace,
   That one short hour was told.

STEPHEN PHILLIPS.

XII.

THOU who hast follow'd far with eyes of love
  The shy and virgin sights of Spring to-day,
Sad soul, what dost thou in this happy grove ?
  Hast thou no pipe to touch, no strain to play,
Where Nature smiles so fair and seems to ask a
    lay ?

Ah, she needs none ! she is too beautiful.
  How should I sing her ? for my heart would tire,
Seeking a lovelier verse each time to cull,
  In striving still to pitch my music higher :
Lovelier than any Muse is she who gives the fire !

No impulse I beseech ; my strains are vile :
  To escape thee, Nature, restless here I rove.
Look not so sweet on me, avert thy smile !
  O cease at length this fever'd breast to move !
I have loved thee in vain ; I cannot speak my
    love.

Here sense with apathy seems gently wed :
   The gloom is starr'd with flowers ; the unseen
       trees
Spread thick and softly real above my head ;
   And the far birds add music to the peace,
In this dark place of sleep, where whispers never
      cease.

Hush, then, my pipe ; vain is thy passion here ;
   Vain is the burning bosom of desire !
Forever hush'd, let me this silence hear,
   As a sad Muse in the melodious choir
Hushes her voice, to catch the happier voices
      by her.

Deep-shaded will I lie, and deeper yet
   In night, where not a leaf its neighbour knows ;
Forget the shining of the stars, forget
   The vernal visitation of the rose ;
And, far from all delights, prepare my heart's
      repose.

Strive how I may, I cannot slumber so :
   Still burns that sleepless beauty on the mind ;
Still insupportable those visions glow ;
   And hark ! my spirit's aspirations find
An answer in the leaves, a warning on the wind.

' O crave not silence thou ! too soon, too sure,
 Shall Autumn come, and through these branch-
   es weep :
Soon birds shall cease, and flowers no more
   endure ;
 And thou beneath the mould unwilling creep,
And silent soon shalt be in that eternal sleep.

' Green still it is, where that fair goddess strays ;
 Then follow, till around thee all be sere.
Lose not a vision of her passing face;
 Nor miss the sound of her soft robes, that here
Sweep over the wet leaves of the fast-falling
   year.'

         MANMOHAN GHOSE.

XIII.

ORESTES.

ME in far lands did Justice call, cold queen
Among the dead, who after heat and haste
At length have leisure for her steadfast voice,
That gathers peace from the great deeps of
    hell.
She call'd me, saying : ' I heard a cry by night !
Go thou, and question not ; within thy halls
My will awaits fulfilment. Lo, the dead
Cries out before me in the under-world.
Seek not to justify thyself : in me
Be strong, and I will show thee wise in time ;
For, though my face be dark, yet unto those
Who truly follow me through storm or shine,
For these the veil shall fall, and they shall see
They walk'd with Wisdom, though they knew
    her not.'
So sped I home ; and from the under-world
Forever came a wind that fill'd my sails,
Cold, like a spirit ! and ever her still voice

Spoke over shoreless seas and fathomless deeps,
And in great calms, as from a colder world ;
Nor slack'd I sail by day, nor yet when night
Fell on my running keel, and now would burn,
With all her eyes, my errand into me.
So sped I on, fill'd with a voice divine :
And hardly wist I whom I was to slay,
My mother ! but a vague, heroic dream
Possess'd me ; fired to do the will of gods,
I lost the man in minister of Heaven ;
Nor took I note of sandbank, nor of storm,
Nor of the ocean's thunders, when the shores
All round had faded, leaving me alone :
I knew I could not die, till I had slain !
But, when I came once more upon the land
That rear'd me, all the sweetness of old days
Came back on me : I stood, as from a dream
Waked to a sudden, sad reality.
And when, far off, I saw those ancient towers,
The palaces and places of my youth,
I long'd to fall into my mother's arms,
And tell a thousand tales of near escapes.
And lo ! the nurse, that fondled me of yore,
Fell with glad tears upon my neck, and told
How she, and how my mother, all this while
Had dream'd of all I was to do, and said
How dear I should be to my mother's eyes.

C

Her words shook me, but shook not my resolve.
For even then there came that sterner voice,
Echoing to what was highest in the soul.
Then, like to those who have a work on earth,
And put far from them lips of wife or child,
And gird them to the accomplishment; so I
Strode in, nor saw at all mine ancient halls;
And struck my father's murderess, not my mother.
And, when I had smitten, lo, the strength of gods
Pass'd from me, and the old, familiar halls
Reel'd back on me; dim statues, that of old
Holding my mother's hand I marvell'd at,
And questioned her of each. And she lies there,
My mother! ay, my mother now; O hair,
That once I play'd with in these halls! O eyes
That for a moment knew me as I came,
And lighten'd up, and trembled into love;
The next, were darken'd by my hand! Ah me!
Ye will not look upon me in that world.
Yet thou, perchance, art happier, if thou go'st
Into some land of wind and drifting leaves,
To sleep without a star; but as for me,
Hell hungers, and the restless Furies wait.
Then the dark Curse, that sits upon the towers,
Bow'd down her awful head, thus satisfied;
And I fled forth, a murderer, through the world.

STEPHEN PHILLIPS.

XIV.

THE SEASONS' COMFORT.

DRY thine eyes, Doll! the stars above us
    shine;
God of His goodness made them mine and thine;
His silver have we gotten, and His gold,
Whilst there's a sun to call us in the morn
To ply the hook amid the yellow corn,
That such a mine of pretty gems doth hold:
For there's the poppy, half in sorrow,
Greeting sleepy-eyed the morrow,
And the corn-flower, dainty tire for a sweetheart
    sunny poll'd.

Dry thine eyes, Doll! the woods are all our own,
The woods that soon shall take a braver tone,
What time the frosts first silver Nature's hair;
The birds shall sing their best for thee and me;
And every sunrise listeners will we be,
And so of singing get the goodliest share;
When the thrushes sing so sweetly,
We would fain be footing featly,
But our hearts dance time instead in the throb-
    bing matin air.

Dry thine eyes, Doll! there's Love to feed our
    fire,
Not for the buying, but for the desire ;
Winter ne'er quench'd a blaze so bravely fed.
And Sleep, I wot, will grudge us not his best :
In winter earlier sink the suns to rest,
And eke the sooner shall our toils be sped ;
When in the embers glowing
There'll be love-charms worth the knowing,
Or, at Yule-tide, mazes threaded, with the mis-
    tletoe o'erhead.

                    ARTHUR S. CRIPPS.

XV.

O SUMMER sun, O moving trees !
   O cheerful human noise, O busy glittering
     street !
What hour shall Fate in all the future find,
Or what delights, ever to equal these :
Only to taste the warmth, the light, the wind,
Only to be alive, and feel that life is sweet ?

LAURENCE BINYON.

XVI.

MENTEM MORTALIA TANGUNT.

NOW lonely is the wood :
    No flower now lingers, none !
  The virgin sisterhood
    Of roses, all are gone ;
Now Autumn sheds her latest leaf :
    And in my heart is grief.

  Ah me, for all earth rears
    The appointed bound is placed !
After a thousand years
    The great oak falls at last :
And thou, more lovely, canst not stay,
    Sweet rose, beyond thy day.

  Our life is not the life
    Of roses and of leaves ;
  Else wherefore this deep strife,
    This pain, our soul conceives ?
The fall of ev'n such short-lived things
    To us some sorrow brings.

And yet, plant, bird, and fly
  Feel no such hidden fire.
Happy they live ; and die
  Happy, with no desire.
They in their brief life have fulfill'd
All Nature in them will'd.

And were we also made
  Of like terrestrial mould,
We should not be afraid,
  Nor feel the grave so cold ;
But, all oblivious of our fate,
Live sweetly out our date.

For the great Mother loves
  Her children far too well ;
These longings that she moves
  Their own fulfilment tell :
She would not burden us with aught
We really needed not.

O, not in vain she gave
  To the wild birds their wings !
They spread them forth, and have
  Heaven for their wanderings.
But we, to whom no wings are given
Why seek we for a Heaven ?

And, when far o'er us fly
Those voyagers of the air,
Why must we gaze, and sigh,
O would that I were there ?
Why are we restless, ill content
Tied to one element ?

'Tis not that in our tears
Some happier life we crave ;
Our happiest, sweetest years
Mysterious moments have :
The sense of our brief human lot
Clings to us, haunts our thought.

O then this pleasant earth
Seems but an alien thing :
Faint grows her busy mirth ;
Far hence our thoughts take wing :
For some enduring home we cry !
She cannot satisfy,

Or bind us : only ties
Immortal found can bless ;
Only in loving eyes
We see our happiness ;
Only upon a loving breast
Our souls find any rest.

Why thirsts the spirit so
  For life ? what moves it thus ?
'Tis *her* voice ; yes, I know,
  'Tis Nature cries in us :
'Tis no unholy strife of ours
Against forbidding powers.

What though we gaze with fear,
  So blank death seems to be ;
What though no land appear
  Beyond that lonely sea ;
Still in our hearts her cry doth stay ;
She will find out a way.

So in the chrysalis
  Slumber those lovely wings ;
So from the shell it is
  The dazzling pearl she brings :
Her glorious works she works alone,
  Unfathom'd, and unknown !

MANMOHAN GHOSE.

D

www.ingramcontent.com/pod-product-compliance
Lightning Source LLC
Chambersburg PA
CBHW022207020726
47496CB00008B/2912